First published in the United States, Great Britain, Canada,
Australia and New Zealand in 1987 by North-South Books, an
imprint of Rada Matija AG.

Distributed in the United States by
Henry Holt and Company, Inc., 521 Fifth Avenue,
New York, New York 10175.
Library of Congress Cataloging in Publication Data

MacDonald, George, 1824–1905.
Daylight.

Summary: At her christening, the princess, Little
Daylight, receives a curse from a wicked fairy that she
shall never see the sun until kissed by a prince.
[1. Fairy tales]   I. Duntze, Dorothée, ill.
II. Title.
PZ8.M1754Day   1987   [E]   87-1561

ISBN 0-8050-0493-9

Distributed in Great Britain by
Blackie and Son Ltd, 7 Leicester Place,
London WC2H 7BP.
British Library Cataloguing in Publication Data

Bell, Anthea
Little daylight.
I. Title   II. MacDonald, George, *1824–1905.*
At the back of the north wind   III. Duntze,
Dorothée
833'.914[J]   PZ7

ISBN 0-200-72912-8

Distributed in Canada by
Editions Etudes Vivantes, Saint-Laurent.

Distributed in Australia and New Zealand by
Buttercup Books Pty. Ltd., Melbourne.
ISBN 0949447579

Printed in Germany

Little Daylight

By George MacDonald

Adapted by Anthea Bell

Illustrated by Dorothée Duntze

North-South Books

One glorious summer morning, a little Princess was born — a beautiful baby, with such bright eyes that she could have come from the sun, and so they called her little Daylight. There was great jubilation in the palace, for this was the first baby the King and Queen had had.

There was a wood near the palace of the King; such a large wood that nobody yet had ever got to the other end of it. Seven good fairies lived in this wood.

But there was another fairy who had lately come to the place. She lived in a mud house, in a swampy part of the forest. A wicked old thing she was, and the people round about thought she was a witch.

Of course all the good fairies were invited to the Princess's christening.
But the wicked fairy came without being asked.

Five fairies had already given the child such gifts as each counted
best, when the wicked fairy hobbled out into the middle of the circle.

"Please, Your Grace, I'm very deaf," she said to the archbishop.
"Would Your Grace mind repeating the Princess's name?"

"With pleasure, my good woman," said the archbishop. "The
infant's name is little Daylight."

"And little daylight it shall be," cried the fairy, "and little good shall
any of her gifts do her. For I bestow upon her the gift of sleeping all day
long, whether she will or not. Ha, ha! He, he! Hi, hi!"

Then out stepped the sixth fairy, to undo as much of the curse as
she might. "If she sleeps all day," she said mournfully, "she shall, at
least, wake all night."

"You spoke before I had finished laughing," said the wicked fairy. "That's against the law. It gives me another chance. I had only got to Hi, hi! and I still had to go through, Ho, ho! and Hu, hu! So I decree that if she wakes all night she shall wax and wane with its mistress the moon. Ho, ho! Hu, hu!"

But out stepped the seventh fairy. "Until a prince comes who shall kiss her without knowing it," she said.

"I don't know what that means," said the poor King to the fairy.

"Don't be afraid. The meaning will come with the thing itself," said she.

So at certain times the palace rang all night with bursts of laughter from little Daylight, whose heart the old fairy's curse could not reach; she was Daylight still, only a little in the wrong place, for she always dropped asleep at the first hint of dawn in the east.

However, her merriment did not last long. When the moon was at the full, she was in glorious spirits, and as beautiful as any child of her age could be. But as the moon waned, she faded, until she was wan and withered as the poorest, sickliest child ever seen. Then the night was quiet as the day, for the little creature lay in her gorgeous cradle hardly moving, without even a moan. At first they often thought she was dead, but at last they got used to it, and waited for her to begin to revive with the silver thread of the crescent moon, and grow better and better.

And so it went on until she was nearly seventeen. Her father and mother had by that time got quite used to the odd state of things. But how any prince was ever to find and deliver her, no one could imagine.

A little way from the palace there was a great open glade, which was Daylight's favourite haunt, for here the full moon shone free and glorious. She had a little rustic house built for her in the glade, and here she mostly lived.

About this time, a young Prince lost his way in the wood. He had been wandering for days when he came to the great glade. He saw the lovely little house, and decided to knock at its door, but then all at once he saw a most beautiful girl, singing like a nightingale and dancing to her own music. As if enchanted, the Prince stepped out into the glade.

When Daylight heard him coming, she stopped and asked, "What do you want? Are you good?"

"Not so good as I should wish to be," said the Prince.

"I like you!" said the Princess. "Can you tell me what the sun is like?"

"Why, it shines like the moon," said the Prince, surprised. "But where's the good of asking what you know?"

"But I don't know! I am Daylight, who can't stay awake in the daytime, and I never shall until..." Here she hid her face in her hands, turned away, and walked slowly towards the house. The Prince was going to follow her, but she turned and waved him away.

Sadly, he went back into the wood, and there the bad fairy found him! She so contrived it, by her deceitful spells, that the next night the Prince could not find his way to the glade. He wandered about the forest for days, trying to find Daylight, for he could not forget her. But the bad fairy had bewitched the wood.

Not until the last quarter of the moon did she stop casting spells, for there was no chance of the Prince wishing to kiss the worn, decrepit creature Princess Daylight became as the moon waned.

Then at last he found the glade again. As the moon was only a thin crescent in the sky, it was very dark, and the Prince thought that if he lit a fire, Daylight might see it and come to him. His fire was just beginning to blaze up, when he heard a moan. He sprang to his feet, and found a human form, with a face like that of an old woman, lying on the ground. The Prince took off his cloak, and wrapped it about the old woman. Then he took her in his arms, to carry her to the Princess's house, and she gave such a sad moan that it went to his very heart. "Poor thing!" he said softly, and kissed her on the withered lips.

Suddenly she slipped from his arms, and stood upright on her feet. Her hood had dropped, and her hair fell about her. The first gleam of the morning was caught on her face. The Prince could hardly believe his eyes. It was Daylight herself whom he had brought out of the forest.

"You kissed me when you thought I was an old woman: there! I kiss you now I am a young princess," murmured Daylight. "Is that the sun coming?"